The
Littles
and the Surprise
Thanksgiving Guests

To the memory of my father, John Peterson,
who was the first to discover the Littles
and write of their adventures

ISBN 0-439-68704-7

Text copyright © 2004 by Joel Peterson.
Illustrations copyright © 2004 by Scholastic Inc.
All rights reserved. Published by Scholastic Inc.

SCHOLASTIC and associated logos are trademarks
and/or registered trademarks of Scholastic Inc.

12 11 10 9 8 7 6 5 4 3 2 1   4 5 6 7 8 9/0

Printed in the U.S.A.   40
First printing, November 2004

The
Littles
and the Surprise
Thanksgiving Guests

by **Joel Peterson**
Pictures by **Roberta Carter Clark**
Cover illustration by **Jacqueline Rogers**

A
LITTLE APPLE
PAPERBACK

SCHOLASTIC INC.
New York Toronto London Auckland Sydney
Mexico City New Delhi Hong Kong Buenos Aires

Tom and Lucy Little sat together, wrapped in a small, red bandana to protect themselves from the cool October air. The two tiny children were on the roof of the Biggs' house, huddled against the warm chimney. It was late in the afternoon on Halloween day, and they were doing something they liked to do every year at this time: They were watching trick-or-treaters.

From the rooftop, Lucy and Tom could see children dressed up in costumes on the street below. The trick-or-treaters were running from house to house, ringing doorbells, shouting and laughing, as their bags of candy grew more and more full. Tom and Lucy were pointing out their favorite costumes to each other. They got just as big a kick out of the holiday as the children down in the street.

"If I had a Halloween costume," eight-year-old Lucy Little said, "I'd be a ladybug. I'd be little and shiny and red. I'd have black polka dots all over me, and two wings that flapped when I pulled on a hidden string!"

"Oh, yeah?" her ten-year-old brother, Tom, said with a grin. "It's funny you picked *that* for a costume. I was just thinking that if *I* were going trick-or-treating, I'd dress up as a big, black, hairy spider. I'd have eight fuzzy, pipe-cleaner arms and a furry spider body made from an old wool sock . . ." Tom leaned in toward his sister, ". . . and we all know what spiders like to eat, don't we?"

Lucy looked at her brother with a puzzled expression.

"Ladybugs!" shouted Tom. He grabbed her shoulders and laughed.

Lucy jumped. "Tom Little!" she scolded. "You just about scared the heck out of me! Besides, that's not even true! Spiders do *not* eat ladybugs! They eat flies — *everyone* knows that!"

"Oh, really?" said Tom. "Do you remember last spring when those ladybugs were all over the neighborhood, and some of them got into the house?"

Lucy nodded.

Tom went on: "I was playing in Henry Bigg's room while Henry was at school, and do you know what I saw?"

Lucy gulped and shook her head.

"I saw a big, fat spider in a web in the corner of the room. And do you know what he was doing?"

Again, Lucy shook her head. Her eyes grew wider.

"He had a big bowl of ladybugs, and he was shelling them like peanuts! He was reading a little newspaper with two of his arms. He was shelling the ladybugs with two *different* arms and eating them with two *other* arms. Then, he was tossing the shells over his shoulders into a neat little pile with his *last* two arms!"

At the end of his story, Tom fell over laughing. His sister smacked Tom's arm and pretended to be angry. But she was laughing at the ridiculous story, too, and at herself for falling for it.

Tom and Lucy Little were not just brother and sister; they were the best of friends and constant companions.

They were the oldest children of Mr. and Mrs. William T. Little. Everyone in their family was tiny. Mr. Little stood just six inches high. But, among the tiny family and their friends, he was considered to be rather tall! Tom and Lucy's baby sister,

Betsy, was *so* small that she could easily sleep in the palm of your hand.

The Littles were House Tinies. Their rooms were snugly nestled between the inside and outside walls of an old house owned by a regular-size family named the Biggs. Mr. and Mrs. George Bigg and their son, Henry, had no idea that the Littles lived there. Not one of these tiny people had ever been seen by a regular-size person.

UNCLE PETE

UNCLE NICK

On the other hand, the Littles' entire lives depended on the Bigg family. They ate from the Biggs' leftovers and made clothing from the Biggs' cast-offs. They even entertained themselves by secretly watching the television shows that the Bigg family watched each night.

GRANDPA

In return for what they took, the Littles

DELLA   DINKY

kept the workings of the Biggs' house in tip-top condition. They took special care of the plumbing and electrical systems. They did such a good job that Mr. Bigg often wondered how it was possible that such an old house needed so few repairs.

Even though the Littles were very, very small, they looked and acted just like any one of us might look and act . . . with *one* rather important difference. They had tails — sleek, glossy, beautiful tails!

Their tails weren't useful. Tiny people couldn't wag them or hang by them. But the tiny people were very proud of them anyhow. Both men and women kept their tails spotlessly groomed. In fact, some tiny women and girls wore ribbons and bows on their tails. Mrs. Little herself, it is well known, must brush her tail one hundred times each night before she goes to bed.

The sun was beginning to set over the Big Valley. Tom and Lucy watched as the last of the afternoon's skeletons, ghosts, vampires, and princesses wandered across the yards and sidewalks below. Suddenly, Tom squinted into the bright orange and red autumn sunset. Something was flying toward them from the direction of the setting sun — and it was coming fast!

"Lucy, do you see that?" Tom shouted. "It's flying too smoothly to be a bird, but the sun's so bright I can't tell for sure *what* it is." As the object drew closer, the two children could clearly see its black silhouette against the blazing sky.

"It's Cousin Dinky! He's flying his new glider!" exclaimed Lucy, jumping up. "It's the toy glider that Mr. Bigg built in his basement workshop for Henry! He threw it out because he couldn't get it to work right, but Cousin Dinky fixed it! Oh, I knew he could!"

"If it *is* Cousin Dinky," said Tom, "he's flying much too fast to make a safe landing. He'll crash for sure if he tries!"

The glider flew rapidly toward them. Whoever was at the controls wasn't even going to try landing on the roof. The craft zoomed over them, passing a mere few feet away from their heads. Suddenly, the left-hand wing tipped down toward the roof of the house, and the children could see the pilot very clearly.

Their jaws dropped open. Instead of their adventurous, daredevil Cousin Dinky, they saw a big, furry, river rat flying the glider! The rat turned toward the startled children, placed a paw to its forehead, and saluted!

Tom and Lucy looked at one another. Their mouths were still open in shock. When they looked back at the glider, its wings were clipping the very top of the maple tree in the front yard. This sent a blizzard of brilliantly colored leaves flying in every direction.

The leaves settled gently in the yard below as the glider climbed higher and higher. For a moment it seemed to hang in midair. Just then it arched over backward, into a gigantic loop-de-loop. Then the glider straightened out and came in for a landing on the roof.

The rat pilot released two parachutes from the rear of the glider to slow the craft down. As the glider bounced along the rooftop, the rat threw out a fish-hook anchor, tied to a piece of twine.

The hook caught the shingles of the rooftop, and the glider stopped with a jerk. It was such a hard jerk that the pilot's seat, with the rat still belted into it, popped out. The seat skidded along the rooftop and came to a screeching halt right in front of Tom and Lucy. The children's mouths were still hanging wide open.

The rat pilot shook his head. "Stupid ejector seat!" he muttered. "Still has a few bugs to be worked out." Then he grabbed his ears and yanked off his own head! The children suddenly found themselves face to face with their favorite cousin, Dinky Little. "Trick or treat!" he shouted, as he tossed the rat-head mask to Tom.

"Cousin Dinky!" cried Lucy. She ran over to her cousin and gave him a hug. "Where's Della?"

"The little woman is home keeping the home fires burning," Dinky said. Then he laughed at his "little" pun. "Now give me a hand getting out of this dang-blasted contraption, and let's go downstairs. I have some wonderful news!"

Tom, Lucy, and Dinky made their way from the rooftop down to the Littles' apartment through a secret trapdoor shingle. They walked through a maze-like series of passageways that were hidden behind the walls of the old house.

The Littles had long ago made their own elevators from soup cans, strings, and pulleys in order to get from floor to floor. They knew the spaces behind the walls like they knew the backs of their own hands. They could go from one end of the Biggs' house to the other in a matter of minutes.

The Littles' apartment was very cozy. They had bedrooms and a very nice living room. The Littles had also built a bath-room and a kitchen. The kitchen didn't have much in the way of appliances, but none were really needed. The Littles more often than not ate whatever was left over from the Biggs' dinner table.

The furniture in the apartment had been cleverly created from household objects and various items that the Biggs had thrown out over the years. The Littles' living room even *looked* a bit like the Biggs' living room, as the Littles had borrowed some of the leftover paint and carpet scraps after Mrs. Bigg had finished redecorating *her* home!

As the Little children and their cousin got to the door of their family's apartment, Tom pulled on Cousin Dinky's sleeve. "Hey, Cousin Dinky! Put your mask back on — let's throw a scare into everyone for Halloween!"

Dinky was still a kid at heart, and couldn't resist a good practical joke. "What the heck!" he laughed. He popped on the river rat costume head.

Tom Little threw open the door to the apartment. "Hey, everyone! Look what Lucy and I found up on the roo —"

Before he could finish the sentence, his uncle, Major Nick Little, had jumped to his feet. In a flash, he pulled a tiny, sharp dagger from his shiny, black boot. He hurled it through the air, pinning the left shoulder of Dinky's costume to the door.

Lucy let out a loud scream. "Uncle Nick — *No*! It's just Cousin Dinky!" she cried.

Dinky had very quickly taken the mask off, and was staring at his uncle in disbelief. Uncle Nick was speechless, his face drained of color. He rushed over to Dinky and pulled the dagger out of his costume.

The others in the room — Mr. Little, Mrs. Little, and the children's Uncle Pete — all sat frozen in their seats, too shocked to move. Luckily, Granny and

Grandpa Little were in another room, playing with Baby Betsy. They both might have had heart attacks.

"Sweet-Jumping-Jiminy-in-the-Morning! Nick, have you gone completely mad?" shouted Uncle Pete. "You could have hurt Tom or Lucy . . . and you could have *killed* Dinky!"

"I'm *so* sorry! I'm so *terribly* sorry!" Uncle Nick said as he put his arm around Cousin Dinky's shoulder. He hugged Tom and Lucy and kept apologizing. Then he squeezed all their arms and elbows to be sure they were still in one piece.

Later, after everyone had calmed down, the family sat together in the Littles' living room. Dinky had taken off his costume. He was sitting on the sofa in his long johns, drinking a mug of very strong, very hot, black coffee.

"Once again, Dinky, I must apologize," Uncle Nick was saying. "We weren't expecting you, and certainly not all done up in a Halloween costume. After all, you're a grown man, and one doesn't expect that sort of thing from an adult."

Uncle Pete chuckled. "Speaking of adults behaving in a strange manner, Nick, old fellow, I didn't know you still had it in you! Why, I remember the days when there wasn't a mouse in the entire Big Valley that was safe from Major Nicholas T. Little! Your reflexes are very nearly everything they used to be."

"Well, I'm glad they aren't *everything* they used to be," said Dinky as he took a sip of coffee, rubbed his throat, and looked in Uncle Nick's direction. "If he still had it in *him*, I might have had it in *me*!"

Major Nick Little started pacing up and down. As usual, he was dressed neatly in his major's uniform.

"It's not all my fault, is it?" he said. "After all, mice and rats are no laughing matter to us older tinies. The Great Mouse Invasion may be a grand old story to you younger folks, but I" — he paused and waved his hand toward Uncle Pete — "*we* actually *lived* through those troubled times. Why do you think Pete here limps and walks with a cane? Because of an old hopscotch accident? No — he came face-to-face with a set of sharp, cruel mouse teeth. I was there on that terrible day. Let me tell you, it's a miracle that he's even got two legs today."

Uncle Nick took a breath. "We fought side by side with a lot of good men. Some of them weren't lucky enough to live to tell the tale."

Uncle Nick wiped a tear from the corner of his eye. "As a Major in the Mouse Brigade in Trash City, I saw things over the course of my thirty-year service that would make the flesh melt right off your bones!"

His voice grew louder, and his cheeks flushed red as he continued. "And I didn't make a career out of protecting a lot of very good people from vicious vermin just to be the butt of some young people's foolish Halloween prank!"

Mrs. Little put her arm around Uncle Nick's shoulders. "Please calm down, Nick," she said softly. "It isn't like you to get so upset over something like this."

Uncle Nick looked at her and sighed. "I'm sorry. I'm sorry, everyone. Something *has* been bothering me lately. It sounds foolish, I know, but this cold weather we've been having makes me nervous.

This fall feels *exactly* like it did right before the Great Mouse Invasion."

He thought back to that fateful time. "It was the brutal early cold spell that drove all of the mice indoors that year. I know this is only the end of October, but there's a feeling in the air that's just the same. Believe me, after so many years of paying attention to this sort of thing, one gets a nose for it."

Uncle Nick pointed to a Mouse War medal on his chest. "And I didn't get *this*, or lose *this*," he pulled off his false tail, and tossed it at Lucy, "by not knowing my business. I don't pussy-foot around when it comes to mice!"

Lucy giggled. "Ick!" she squealed. She quickly picked up her uncle's false tail. She held it out as though it were a snake, and tossed it back to him, laughing all the while.

"Say, Cousin Dinky — what's your great news?" Tom asked his cousin.

Dinky looked up from his coffee. "Oh!

How could I forget? That's the very reason I came!" He put his coffee mug down.

"A few months ago, Della and I flew into the Great Woods to deliver your Thanksgiving invitation to our old Tree Tiny friend, Stubby Speck. We found him fishing for minnows along the bank of the creek. He must have had five fishing lines going at once!"

"Five lines! Holy smoke!" Mr. Little whistled. "How on earth did he manage that? After all, Stubby only has two arms."

"Well," Cousin Dinky explained, "he had three poles stuck in the gooey muck by the side of the creek, and two lines tied to each of his big toes. He was resting on a soft bed of thick, green moss down by the water's edge. He was leaning against his sidekick, Old Skunk. They were both snoring away like old pick-up trucks with broken mufflers."

Mr. Little laughed. "Sounds just like Stubby."

"We woke Stubby up," Dinky said. "You

know the old expression — it's best to let sleeping skunks lie."

"You're right there," said Uncle Pete.

"Anyway," Cousin Dinky went on, "Stubby said the Speck family would be delighted to come here for Thanksgiving dinner. His wife and daughters have been dying to get out of the tree, and they're all very excited to visit a real house."

Like all Tree Tinies, the Specks lived in rooms inside a hollow tree trunk.

"Stubby suggested that they stay the entire week and have a good visit. We figured that would be fine, and we told him so."

Dinky sipped his coffee, and waited to see what Mrs. Little said. Maybe she would be angry that he and Della had invited the Specks to stay for such a long time.

"Thanksgiving week! What a wonderful idea!" Mrs. Little smiled. "That gives us plenty of time to get things ready."

Dinky breathed a sigh of relief.

The rest of the Littles were glad to have company, particularly Tom and Lucy. They were always excited to have a chance to play with other tiny children.

Everyone began to talk at once. Granny and Grandpa Little came out of the room where Baby Betsy's cradle was kept.

"What's all the hubbub about out here?" asked Granny. "We just got Betsy to fall asleep, and all this racket's sure to wake her up!" She suddenly noticed Cousin Dinky sitting with the rest of the family. "Dinky Little! Goodness sakes alive! Nobody told me you were coming!"

She looked him up and down. "And sitting there in your *underwear*! Why, it's disgraceful that a man of your age—"

She suddenly let out a loud shriek, and fainted dead away. Grandpa Little caught her before she fell on the floor. Granny had seen the river rat full-head mask lying on the sofa next to Dinky.

Grandpa Little stared at the rest of the family. He looked very confused.

Tom and Lucy Little looked at one another. Tom sighed and shrugged his shoulders. "Here we go again!" he said. Lucy just shook her head.

Two weeks after Cousin Dinky's visit, Lucy Little decided to go down into the Biggs' basement. She wasn't supposed to go there by herself, but she would often sneak down anyway.

She loved to watch Mr. Bigg as he worked at his hobby. He created many beautiful objects out of wood. Lucy's favorites were the wonderful toys that he made for his son Henry.

When Lucy got down to the basement, she made her way to a dark little room the Biggs called the root cellar. A hot water pipe that ran right through the root cellar made a good observation platform for a tiny. Lucy lay down on the pipe. From there, she could see into the room next door through the hole in the wall where the pipe passed through.

Mr. Bigg was sanding a small wooden bear figurine he had made. When he was done, he placed it carefully inside of a large, mysterious, striped tent that covered most of his workbench.

"There you go, buddy," he said to the bear, "you can just relax in there with the rest of your pals 'til next time. I'm calling it a night." Mr. Bigg yawned and sat back in his chair.

Lucy was disappointed. "Oh, well," she thought, "it's freezing cold down here anyway." She stood up and started to walk back along the pipe. Suddenly, she heard the sound of glass breaking.

"No wonder it's so cold," she thought. "The basement window is falling apart."

Then, without warning, four field mice burst through the window of the root cellar. They landed right on the pipe in front of Lucy. She didn't move a muscle. The biggest mouse turned its head and stared right at her.

The other mice slowly turned their heads as well. Their eyes looked mean and cruel to Lucy, like hungry sharks' eyes might look.

Without thinking, Lucy turned around and ran back the way she had come. The mice ran after her. Lucy squeezed through the hole that the pipe ran through, and right into Mr. Bigg's workroom!

She stopped and looked back. One of the biggest mice was struggling to squeeze through the hole after Lucy. When it popped through, it charged directly at her! She ran for her life.

Mr. Bigg heard them scrambling on the pipe over his head. "Darn cold weather's bringing mice indoors!" he grumbled. He sounded angry. He stood up and smacked the pipe with a yardstick. Lucy was almost all the way across the pipe.

A few inches away was the door to another secret passageway that the Littles sometimes used. Lucy stopped and looked back when she heard the yardstick hit the pipe. It hit just in front of the attacking mouse. The mouse was so startled that it fell off the pipe and onto the basement floor!

Mr. Bigg ran after the mouse, but it squeezed through a hole in the basement wall. Then Mr. Bigg looked up into the darkness where Lucy was standing. He squinted his eyes.

"It may be dark up there," he said, "but I can see your beady little eyes looking at me. Enjoy your life while you can, you furry little beast, because it isn't going to be a very long one!"

Lucy turned and ran. Just as she got to the secret door, Mr. Bigg turned his table light upside down, and shone it on the basement ceiling.

"Now I see you. I can see your tail, you dirty little rat!" he said, as Lucy disappeared.

Later, in her family's apartment, Lucy told her family what had happened. Her mother had to give her a cup of hot chocolate to calm her down.

"We're about to have a house full of unwelcome and very dangerous visitors," said Uncle Nick. "We need to fix that window, and fast!"

"I'm sure that Mr. Bigg won't let the window stay broken for very long," Mrs. Little said hopefully.

"I'm not so sure," said Mr. Little. "I know the window Lucy's talking about. It's in a basement room that the Biggs never use. The window can't be seen from the outside of the house, either. It's under the deck that Mr. Bigg built out back. He would have to lie down on the patio in the backyard just to see the window."

Mr. Little shook his head. "No, he'd never even know there was a problem until this winter, when the water pipes freeze solid and burst. I'm afraid by the time that happens, this house will be completely filled with hungry mice. Uncle Nick is right. We're going to have to fix that window ourselves — and *quickly*. Until we do, it's an open invitation for every rodent that passes by to come in and keep warm."

"What about Hildy?" asked Lucy. Hildy was the Biggs' cat. She was their friend. She sometimes let the Littles ride on her back.

"Hildy's no spring chicken anymore, Lucy," said Uncle Pete. "Besides," he shot a sideways glance at Uncle Nick, "Hildy's days as a great mouser have pretty much been over ever since a certain *someone* introduced her to a certain tamed pet mouse of his, and she learned to love the enemy! No, forget about the cat straightening this mess out. It's like your father says: Window fixed, problem solved."

"I hope so," Mrs. Little fretted. "After all, it's not just *our* safety we have to worry about now. We have houseguests coming very soon."

"Don't worry, dear." Mr. Little walked over and hugged his wife. "We'll get the window fixed right away. No more mice are going to get indoors. We'll have a wonderful Thanksgiving visit with our friends, and the Specks will have a terrific time, you just wait and see!"

Mr. Little's words made Mrs. Little feel safe and warm. Still, she couldn't help but notice that he was shaking ever so slightly. She could also feel his heart pounding very quickly as he held her tightly in his arms.

"See? There's the hole that the mice are using to get into the house!" Lucy was pointing at a large broken section of window in the Biggs' basement root cellar. Mr. Little, Uncle Nick, Tom, and Uncle Pete stood on the stone windowsill next to her.

Tom carried a backpack that contained some items he thought they might need. One was a small tube of super-strong quick-drying glue. It was the kind of glue made especially for repairing glass objects. They had found it in Mr. Bigg's workshop.

Mr. Little and Uncle Pete both wore swords in their belts. They had been made from two of Mrs. Bigg's sharpest and longest sewing needles.

Uncle Nick carried a very special weapon. It was a genuine officer's saber. It had been hand-fashioned by the best tiny blacksmiths in Trash City. The gleaming edge was made from pieces of three unused razor blades.

When Uncle Nick gripped the wooden handle and pulled the sword from its leather sheath, his hand was protected inside of a beautifully engraved antique thimble of pure silver. The saber had been presented to Uncle Nick for his years of outstanding service when he retired from Trash City's Mouse Brigade. The presenter was none other than the city's newest leader herself, Mayor Julie Annie.

Mr. Little looked down at the pieces of broken glass at his feet. "Fixing this window is going to be a big job, but we can do it," he said. "All of these broken pieces can be glued back together just like a jig-saw puzzle. Then we should be able to stick the whole glued-together piece right back into the hole in the window. If we can find all of the pieces, it should be a perfect fit."

"Right," said Uncle Nick. "After that, we'll reinforce it with some heavy cardboard and duct tape. We need to make sure that the mice can't break through again."

The tiny people scattered all over the window ledge and started picking up the bits of glass. The windowsill was long, and very deep. It was dusty and dirty. One by one, the broken bits of glass were found and carried over near the hole in the window.

Uncle Pete's job was to match the pieces together. As he placed the pieces on the sill, he would stop and scratch his head as he thought about how to fit them against one another.

Finally, the tiny people had found almost every piece. They still needed a single triangle of glass that was about two inches long and half an inch wide. It didn't seem to be anywhere on the ledge at all.

Just when they were about to give up, Uncle Nick shouted, "I found it!" The others ran over and joined him. He was peering over the edge of the stone windowsill.

"There," he said, pointing downward. The missing piece was resting on a dust-covered shelf about two feet below them.

Before anyone could blink, Lucy Little ran over and slid down a copper pipe that ran along the cellar wall. She jumped off and landed on the shelf. A puff of dust rose up around her, and she sneezed loudly. She picked up the piece of glass. "I've got it!" she called out. "Now I just have to shimmy back up the pipe!"

"How do you figure you're going to do that with that hunk of window pane in your hands?" asked Tom.

"Oh," Lucy frowned. "I didn't really think that far ahead." Suddenly, she let out an ear-piercing scream.

"*Mice!*" yelled Uncle Pete. He pointed wildly with his cane.

Everyone looked in horror to see three sleek, lean mice running along the shelf. They were headed straight for Lucy.

The sound of the mice's feet on the wood and the scratching of their claws filled Lucy Little with fear. She spun around and saw the mice moving closer. They were sniffing the air all around Lucy. Their shiny, coal-black eyes darted back and forth as they studied her.

Lucy whirled around in a circle, slashing out at the mice with the piece of glass. The mice squealed and pulled back when she caught the tip of a pink nose, or one of their ears with the sharp edge of the glass. But they didn't run away; they kept on attacking the tiny girl.

"Hang on, Lucy!" yelled Uncle Nick, drawing his saber. "We're coming down to rescue you!" Mr. Little and Uncle Pete both drew their swords, quickly looking about to see if there was another way down to the shelf.

"Tom!" Mr. Little called out. "Where's Tom?"

"I'm up here!" Tom yelled out.

The men looked up, but they couldn't see Tom. He had climbed up the copper tube, and leapt onto the top of the water pipe when the mice had attacked his sister.

Now he took off his backpack, and pulled out a small bungee cord.

"Lucy! Can you hear me?" Tom shouted to his sister in the darkness below.

"Yes! I can hear you! Help me!" She kept spinning around, slashing at the mice with the piece of glass. "Hurry!"

Tom picked up the bungee cord and threw it straight up into the air as hard as he could. The hook at one end caught onto a small pipe that was about a foot over his head. The other end of the cord dangled in front of him.

Tom put his foot in the hook and tied it with a piece of string. He yelled again to his sister.

"Lucy, listen to me carefully. You need to trust what I'm about to tell you. Don't think — just trust me. When I say 'now,' put the glass down and stand very still. Ready?"

Lucy nodded. She was terrified.

"Now!" Tom yelled. Lucy barely had time to set the glass down on the shelf before she was swept off her feet. Tom had swooped down and snatched her up by the arms. They went flying through the air above the heads of the surprised mice.

Lucy and Tom swung back up on top of the water pipe. They landed softly on their feet.

Tom untied his foot. He grabbed Lucy by her hand.

"Let's get out of here!" he said.

They ran as fast as they could.

"How's Lucy doing now?" Mr. Little asked his wife. He was sitting in their bedroom. It was late in the evening, and Mrs. Little had just come back into the room. She had been checking to see how their children were doing after the terrifying events of the day.

"She's finally sleeping," whispered Mrs. Little. "For a while there, I thought that she was going to go into shock, but she's a very brave little girl. I think that she's going to be all right."

Mrs. Little sat down on the bed next to her husband. "Speaking of brave kids, did you have a talk with Tom?"

"I did," said Mr. Little. "I told him that

what he did was dangerous. Bungee jumping! He could have been badly hurt."

"What *else* did you tell Tom?" asked Mrs. Little.

"What *could* I tell him? He saved Lucy's life. He risked his own neck with no thought for his own safety. I want to be angry with him for being so reckless, but I can't. I'm very proud of what Tom did . . . and I told him so."

"That's good," said Mrs. Little. "I'm proud of *both* of our children. It's good to know that in tough times they can be so helpful and fearless."

"We've raised two great kids," Mr. Little agreed. He paused for a moment, then said, "I've been thinking about what happened in the basement today. I've decided that we should wait until the Specks get here before we try to fix the window again. The more tinies we have working at the same time, the better. The ones who aren't actually putting the window back together can help by standing guard while the rest of us fix it. Does that sound like too much to ask of our houseguests?"

"No, I think that's a fine idea," said Mrs. Little. She looked down at the bedspread for a moment, and then up at her husband. "Will, there's something else that I need to tell you," she whispered. "Something that you're not going to like to hear. It's not good at all. I know that more bad news is the last thing that you want to hear right now, but I just *have* to tell someone."

"What is it?" Mr. Little looked at his wife with concern.

"I heard Mr. and Mrs. Bigg talking this afternoon while everyone was down in the basement. They were talking about all the mice they've seen in the house lately. They were saying that they've wanted to get Henry a dog for some time now. They could make Henry happy and get rid of the mice in the house at the same time. They want to get him a terrier as a present on Thanksgiving Day."

"Hmmmm," Mr. Little said. "A terrier, huh?"

"They called it a rat-dog," Mrs. Little said, "a natural enemy of rats and mice. Mr. Bigg said that sort of dog will go after any little creature with a tail. Once the animal is in its teeth, the dog shakes it into little bits!" Mrs. Little looked very upset.

Mr. Little looked troubled as well. "You're right, that *isn't* good news," he said. "I don't think that we should mention this to anyone until they actually bring the dog home. After all, everybody has enough to worry about right now."

Mrs. Little agreed with her husband. They both got ready for bed. "I just know I'm going to lie awake all night worrying," said Mrs. Little.

Her husband sighed as he turned off the light. "I feel the same way," he said. "Goodnight."

They were both so tired, they fell sound asleep the moment their heads touched their pillows.

"When are the Specks going to get here?" Lucy Little asked. It was the same question she had been asking all day. Right now, Lucy was sitting cross-legged in the middle of the living room floor. She was spinning a single jack around and around like a top.

"Soon," her mother told her. "You have to be patient a bit longer."

Granny Little and Lucy's mother were sitting together on the sofa. Granny was knitting a tiny wool hat for Baby Betsy.

Mr. Little and Grandpa Little were playing a card game that Grandpa had invented.

The game was called "Whompers." Grandpa had hand-drawn each tiny playing card himself. He had also built the card table. He had carefully glued together a few playing cards from a normal-sized, antique deck of cards for the tabletop. The surface of the table was a beautiful, laughing Joker card. The table had folding bobby pin legs, so it could be easily stored away when it wasn't being used. Grandpa Little was very proud of his craftsmanship.

"I thought the Specks were coming *today*!" Lucy was very eager to see Janie and Annie Speck. She hadn't seen them since her family had traveled to pay the Speck family a visit at their tree home in the heart of the Great Woods. It seemed like a long time ago to Lucy.

The Specks lived much differently than the Littles did. They didn't have any big people around and had to do everything themselves. Still, their home was very beautiful and their lives were as rich and interesting as that of any House Tiny.

The Littles had met the Specks on one of their many adventures. They had been welcomed into the Tree Tinies' home like members of the Specks' own family.

"They're not going to arrive during the day, Lucy," said her father, looking up from his game. "Remember Stubby Speck's friend Old Skunk?"

Lucy nodded. How could she forget the wild animal that the Specks had managed to tame and train as a family pet?

"Well," her father continued, "Mr. and Mrs. Speck and their daughters are traveling courtesy of Old Skunk's back. He's big enough that they can easily bring whatever else they need along with them. Old Skunk is a nocturnal creature, and that means that he's really only comfortable going out at night. Besides, it's best that they travel under cover of darkness, don't you think?"

Lucy nodded her head again. "Will Old Skunk be staying here, too?" she asked.

"All I know," Mrs. Little chimed in with a smile, "is that I am *not* setting an extra place at our Thanksgiving table for that stinky beast!"

"No," Mr. Little said, "Old Skunk won't be joining us for dinner! In fact, Cousin Dinky told me that the Specks were planning to send him back to the Great Woods after they get here."

"Won't he get lost?" asked Lucy. She looked puzzled.

"Not Old Skunk," Mr. Little said. "He knows the woods like the back of his paw. It's just about time for him to go into hibernation, anyway. He has to get back to his den so he can start his long winter's nap."

"How are the Specks going to get back home after Thanksgiving if Old Skunk doesn't wake up?" Lucy wanted to know.

"He doesn't need to wake up, Lucy. We're going to give the Speck family a ride home after their visit. I'm sure that Hildy won't mind taking everyone back into the woods, especially with your brother Tom doing the driving. That cat just loves that boy."

"Hmph!" Granny Little snorted, looking up from what she was doing. "Tinies riding around on skunks and cats! It just isn't natural!"

"*Whompers*!" yelled Grandpa. He startled everyone in the room as he threw down his cards on Joker's face on the center of his table. "I *won*!"

"Darn it, Dad! You *always* win," said Mr. Little. "In fact, I'm not even sure *how* you won. You make up new rules every time we play!"

"Well, that's the way the cookie crumbles," said Grandpa Little, winking at his wife. "Maybe next time we can play a game that *you* invented, and *you* can see what it feels like to win for a change!"

"Tsk! Oh, Amos, *really*! Isn't it time you grew up?" Granny Little couldn't help chuckling as she scolded her husband. She smiled to herself as she shook her head and went back to her knitting.

"Oh, Tom, look at the moon! Awesome!" Lucy and Tom Little, along with their father, were on the Biggs' back deck. The Specks would be arriving that night, and the three of them had gone out to be the welcoming party.

The Littles had used the secret door that was hidden behind an outdoor electrical socket. The door was just above the floor of the deck.

Mr. Little looked up and whistled. "That moon *is* a beauty, Lucy. See that red ring around it? That means that it's very cold up there."

"It's not so warm down *here*," said Tom, pulling his winter coat closer to himself.

Granny Little had made it from one of Henry Bigg's mittens after Henry lost the other one.

Lucy agreed. "Tom's right. I'm freezing! I hope the Specks get here soon."

"Shhhhhhh! Listen!" Their father held a finger to his lips. Tom and Lucy stopped talking and stood very still. The three tiny people could hear a rustling sound below them, followed by lots of scratching and squeaking.

They looked down toward the Biggs' cement patio.

Tom, Lucy, and Mr. Little could scarcely believe their eyes. There in the moonlight, three feet below them, dozens of mice were running about. They were scurrying under the deck and darting back out again.

"They must be going in and out of the hole in the basement window," Mr. Little said. "I wonder why there are so many of them here in one spot? It's strange. It can't be just because of the broken window.

They keep coming back outside after they've been inside. They're running back and forth."

"I know why, Dad," said Lucy. She pointed.

Lucy's father and brother looked where she was pointing. Mrs. Bigg's birdfeeder hung from an iron pole that came up from the ground. The feeder was overflowing with birdseed, and the seed had spilled all over the patio.

"The mice are eating the birdfeed!" whispered Tom.

No sooner had Tom spoken than the mice stopped eating. They turned their heads and began sniffing the night air. As quickly as lightning, all of the mice disappeared into the shadows.

"I wonder what scared them off?" Tom asked. "Do you think they smelled us?"

"No," said Mr. Little. "The wind is blowing toward us. They couldn't have smelled us. Besides, mice aren't afraid of us. Even if they *were*, they were all so busy eating that I don't think it would have bothered them if they *did* smell us."

"Well, they sure smelled *something*," said Tom.

"Look! Look! They're *here*! The Specks are *here*!" Lucy jumped up and down and started pulling on Tom's arm. She was yelling at the top of her lungs. Her father gave her a stern glance and held his finger to his lips.

"Shhh," he said. "We don't want to wake up the Biggs."

Lucy stopped yelling and began to whisper in an excited voice. "The Specks are *here*! The Specks are *here*!" She was still jumping up and down.

They could just barely make out the shape of Old Skunk. He was padding along out of the woods and into the yard.

"So *that's* what the mice were smelling!" Mr. Little gave a soft laugh. As the big, black-and-white animal got near the Biggs' house, the Littles could clearly see four tiny figures riding on his furry back.

"What's that *behind* Old Skunk, Daddy?" Lucy squinted into the moonlit yard.

"It looks like he's pulling a cart or something," Mr. Little said. "Well, I'll be! It's a covered wagon. They must be bringing a lot of stuff."

As Old Skunk toddled onto the patio, Tom, Lucy, and Mr. Little could hear the voices of the people on the animal's back. They were talking and laughing. Suddenly, the tiny man nearest the front of the skunk let out a loud "*Whoa!*" He pulled gently at the long fur on the skunk's neck, and the plump animal stopped in his tracks.

"You two stay put," Mr. Little said. "I'll go down and help the Specks unload." He turned and headed toward the secret door.

A minute later, the Little children watched as their father made his way toward Old Skunk. They saw him shake hands with Stubby Speck and his wife and the two girls. Then Stubby led Mr. Little to the covered wagon.

"Tom! Who are *they*?" Lucy whispered. Four more tiny people were getting out of the covered wagon!

"It can't be, but it *looks* like the Snippets!" Tom said.

"That's impossible!" Lucy said. "The Snippets are Ground Tinies! They *never* come out of the woods. And they never *ever* come near houses. They're too scared. Everyone knows that."

Just then the four tiny people stepped into the moonlight. It was a man and a woman and two teenage boys.

"It *is* the Snippets!" Tom said. "This is a first!"

Tom and Lucy watched as their father helped the Specks and the Snippets unload the wagon. They had lots of bags. Each of the nine tinies had something to carry. The two Snippet boys then took the wagon's harness off Old Skunk and rolled the wagon under a bush behind the deck.

Mr. Little led the troop toward the drain-pipe doorway under the deck. Old Skunk turned around and headed back into the woods.

"Come on, Lucy," Tom said. "Let's get inside and say hello to everyone. Can you believe it? Tree Tinies *and* Ground Tinies in our house!"

The two Littles turned around and went into the house through the electric socket door.

"Oh, my goodness!" Mrs. Little said, looking around the room. "I just . . . Oh, my *goodness*! I just don't know what to say! I don't know where we're going to put all of these people!"

Grandpa Little looked up from the game of solitaire he was playing at his card table. He let out a long whistle. "Talk about a full house," he said, chuckling to himself. He did a quick count of everyone in the Littles' apartment on the fingers of both hands. When he ran out of fingers, he called Lucy over and she counted out the rest.

She raised seven fingers. Grandpa whistled again. "Seventeen people all under one roof. That's a lot of folks!"

"And don't forget," Tom added, "Cousin Dinky, Della, and Aunt Lily are all coming to stay overnight the day before Thanksgiving. That's only two days away."

"Okay, we can do this," Mrs. Little said, pumping herself up. "We've got some extra beds made up for company. Let's see: Janie and Annie can sleep in Lucy's room, the two Snippet boys can bunk with Tom, Uncle Nick, you can sleep with Uncle Pete — your old army cot must be around here someplace. . . ."

"Me? Share my room with that old coot? Why, I'd sooner sleep in the basement with the *mice*!" Uncle Pete said. He liked to tease his older brother.

Mr. Whit Snippet cleared his throat loudly, and the room grew silent. He turned to Mrs. Little and took off his hat. He held it awkwardly with both hands in front of himself. The tiny man had a beard. He was taller than everyone in the room by at least an inch, and he had to stoop so he wouldn't hit his head on the ceiling. Everyone listened as he spoke.

"We're not wanting to put you good folk to extra trouble, showing up without an invite," he said. "Our friends, the Specks, asked us to come along. We've never forgotten our last adventure together in this place. Ever since then, the Specks and the Snippets like to spend Thanksgiving together."

"Well, I, for one, am glad to see that you two get along," Granny Little said. "I've heard about this feud with the Ground Tinies being against the Tree Tinies and the Tree Tinies hating the Ground Tinies ever since I was a little girl." She stopped talking for a moment. She suddenly had a faraway look in her eyes as she thought about her childhood.

"Of course, in *those* days," she went on, "we all thought that Ground Tinies and Tree Tinies were made-up, make-believe creatures like gnomes and fairies and pixies and such."

"As I be saying," Mr. Snippet continued, "I know it's not polite to show up like this."

"Nonsense!" Mr. Little said. "We hardly ever have company. We're always glad to see old friends. And what better time than Thanksgiving?"

Mrs. Little smiled. "You and your family are just as welcome as you can be, Mr. Snippet. Consider our house your home for the next few days."

Whit Snippet took her hand in his. "Thank you, ma'am. We be having our own sleep-rolls, so don't you worry about where we'll sleep."

He waved his hand at the pile of packages in the middle of the living room floor. "We have also made sure to bring a goodly amount of the food and drink that we folk of the woods enjoy. That way you won't have to do all the cooking. We have plenty to share with everyone. Our womenfolk have been cooking for days."

"Speaking of your . . ." Mrs. Little paused, "*wives*, I know Stubby and his wife, and Annie and Janie — Mr. Snippet, what are your sons' names?"

"This one," Whit Snippet nodded at the older boy, "be Jebadiah, who we call Jeb, and the other one be Cody." Both boys were tall and lanky teenagers. They grinned shyly as their father introduced them to everyone.

Mrs. Little walked over to Mrs. Snippet. She was a very shy, very tiny, very pretty woman, who was half standing behind her husband. "Mrs. Snippet?" she asked, extending her hand. "My name is Wilma. May I ask yours?"

Mrs. Snippet smiled. "It's Kimberly Imogene Marietta Snippet," she said quickly, all in one breath.

"We just call her Kim," said Mr. Snippet. "The whole thing be too long a name, and she be too small for it to fit her."

Everyone in the room laughed and began to feel more relaxed.

"I see that the color's coming back to old Whit's face," said Stubby Speck. He gave Mr. Snippet a friendly slap on the back.

"What do you mean, Stubby?" Mr. Little asked.

"Well, it's like this," said Stubby. He lowered his voice so that the women and children couldn't hear him. "Our brave pal Whit Snippet here was afraid to ride in the wagon behind Old Skunk."

"He was afraid of riding in the wagon?" asked Mr. Little.

"No, no!" laughed Stubby. He looked around to make sure that no one else could hear him. He whispered in Mr. Little's ear. "Whit figured that if anything surprised Old Skunk along the trip, anyone riding back in the wagon would get a big face full of *you-know-what!*"

Mr. Little laughed. "Well, it's been a long day for *everyone*," he said. "I guess it's time to get all the bedding together and find a spot for everyone to sleep."

"Come on, Janie and Annie," Lucy said. "You're staying with me." She led them into her room.

Mrs. Little was helping Mrs. Speck lay out their sleeping bags. "You know, Mrs. Speck," she said, "we've known each other for some time. But I've never learned your name either."

"Oh!" Mrs. Speck laughed. "I guess Stubby never got around to telling you. My name's Ima."

"Ima Speck?" Tom whispered to Lucy. "*Ima Speck*? Is she *joking*?" Lucy reached over and pinched his arm.

"Ow!" Tom was laughing so hard he was accidentally making snorting noises. "What was that for?" He looked at Lucy.

"Because," Lucy scolded her brother, "that's not polite!" Lucy didn't look back at her brother. He noticed that she was pinching her own arm, and trying very hard not to laugh.

On the day before Thanksgiving, Mr. Bigg was at work, and Henry Bigg was at school. Mrs. Bigg was out shopping. The Littles and their guests decided to take advantage of having the house to themselves.

Mrs. Little and Lucy invited Ima Speck, her daughters, and Kim Snippet to take a tour of the Biggs' home. The first stop was the kitchen.

"Let me see if I've got this straight," said Mrs. Speck. "The food comes from a place called a *store*. The big lady puts the food in a huge box that keeps the food cold. When the big people are ready to eat, the big lady makes a fire on that contraption we saw in the corner of the kitchen, and heats the food up. Am I right so far?"

Mrs. Little nodded.

"Then," Mrs. Speck said, "when the big people have eaten their fill, you all run in quick as a weasel and steal the food that they didn't eat, right off their plates."

Mrs. Little laughed. "Well, it's *something* like that, Ima. We don't call it *stealing*. After all, we only take the leftovers. And we don't take anything right in front of the Biggs, for heaven's sake! We manage to take what we need from the kitchen counter when they aren't around. Usually, the rest of the leftovers get thrown away by the Biggs anyway."

Mrs. Snippet shook her head. "Throwing away perfectly good food," she said softly. "That be wasteful."

The tiny women and girls continued their tour of the Biggs' house. They had been walking along one of the many secret passageways in the walls of the house. Mrs. Little pushed on the back of an electrical socket, and the whole panel swung forward. The hidden doorway opened above a bookcase in the Biggs' living room. Mrs. Little, Lucy, Mrs. Snippet, and Mrs. Speck and her daughters walked out onto the wooden bookcase.

"I love times like this," Lucy told her friends, "when all the Biggs are gone. I can go anywhere in the house that I feel like going. I can do *anything* that I want to do! I can scream at the top of my lungs, if I want to."

She walked over to the edge of the bookcase. "*Hello!*" she yelled out to the empty living room. "Hello, Biggs! Hello, world! Lucy Little is here!"

Annie and Janie Speck held their hands over their ears.

"Lucy! Stop showing off and behave yourself!" her mother scolded.

"Watch this!" Lucy said. She ran over to the television remote control that was lying on top of a book. She pounded her tiny fist down on the power button. The Biggs' TV set came to life with a popping sound. The room filled with loud noises.

"It's my favorite cartoon," Lucy said, "*Cosmic Cat*! Look! There's his enemy Kid E. Litter! He's made of *garbage*!" Lucy turned around.

The Speck girls' mouths hung open as they stared at the colorful moving pictures. They'd never even *heard* about television, let alone seen it.

Lucy's mother was giving her a very stern look. Ima Speck and Kim Snippet's heads rose up from behind a box of tissues, where they had quickly hidden when the set came on.

"What be *that*?" Kim Snippet whispered.

Lucy looked where Mrs. Snippet was pointing.

"Oh!" Lucy laughed. "That's just TV. It's the greatest! Look!" She ran over and started stomping on the channel button with her foot.

The tiny women watched as the channels changed. Suddenly the cartoon was gone, and a woman was talking about a new detergent that did a great job cleaning her kid's dirty clothes. Lucy clicked the button again. A newsman was talking about something very sad that had happened to some people in another part of the world. She clicked it again.

"What be *that*?" Mrs. Snippet asked again. Lucy looked at the screen.

"That's just some dumb old movie," said Lucy with a yawn. "It's not even in color."

On the screen, there was a very big, old castle. There were knights in armor standing along the top of the front wall. Hundreds of very angry men were trying to break down the castle's gates. Just as

they had almost succeeded, the knights on
the wall began pouring very large pots of
boiling oil onto the attacking army below.

"No! No! Look out!" shouted Mrs. Speck
at the television set.

"Oh, those poor men!" cried Mrs. Snippet. She hid her face in her hands.

"Don't be afraid," said Lucy. "It's just a stupid movie —" Lucy stopped talking and stared at the screen. Suddenly she turned and ran back toward the electrical socket door. "I've got to go! Bye!" she yelled. Quick as a wink, Lucy Little disappeared into the hidden doorway.

"Lucy Little!" her mother called out. "You come back here this very instant and turn off this television set!"

Lucy was already long gone. Mrs. Little apologized to her friends. "I am *so* sorry," she said. "Honestly, I don't know what's gotten into that girl lately."

She walked over to the remote control and stepped on the power button. The TV screen went black.

At the same time, the tiny men and boys had just finished their own sightseeing trip. They had ended their walking tour of the Bigg house with a visit to Mr. Bigg's basement workshop.

"Over this way," Mr. Little pointed down the pipe, "is the root cellar. That's where we've been having all the trouble that we've told you about. That's where the field mice are coming into the house."

The group of tinies could hear loud chattering and scratching as they got closer to the root cellar.

"We'd better not go in there without any weapons," said Mr. Little. He stopped and sat down on top of the warm water pipe.

"Let's take a rest before we head back upstairs."

The other men sat down along the pipe, dangling their feet high above Mr. Bigg's workbench. They all sat without speaking for a few moments. Uncle Nick, the old military man, was the first one to break the silence.

"Look, we've all agreed that we're going to fix the window. We need to do it while all of you good folks are visiting. Nobody *wants* to do it right now, but there's strength in numbers. Dinky will be here soon. I say we wait for him and then gather up all the weapons we can carry. We come down here, and four of us fix the window while the rest fight off the nasty beasts."

Mr. Snippet shook his head. "We Ground Tinies have never carried weapons," he said. "The way of the weapon not be our way. It never will be. We will be glad to help in the fixing of the glass, but we will not take up arms."

Jeb Snippet spoke up. "Father, if using

weapons will help our friends protect their home, how can it be wrong?"

Whit Snippet raised his voice sharply. "You hush up, boy! It not be *our* way. You know better than that."

Jeb Snippet looked upset, but he just hung his head in silence.

"That's fine, Whit," said Mr. Little. "You don't have to use weapons if you don't believe it's right. But we're going to be in a very dangerous situation here. The possibility of a mouse invasion is a very real problem indeed."

At that very moment, Lucy Little popped out of one of the Littles' secret doorways. She climbed onto the water pipe. She was yelling as she ran along the top of the pipe. "Dad! Tom! *Everyone*! I have a plan! I know how to beat the mice! I know how we can have all the time in the world to fix that window!"

By the time she got to the others, she was breathing hard.

"Settle down, Lucy," said her father. "What's all this about a plan?"

"Well," gasped Lucy, her breath slowly coming back, "I know how we can beat the mice." The tiny group listened to Lucy. They stopped every so often to nod their heads in agreement as she spoke. When Lucy finished talking, Uncle Nick clapped his hands in appreciation.

"Out of the mouths of babes," he said, shaking his head in disbelief. "Lucy Little, I could kiss you. In fact, I *will*!" He walked over and kissed his niece on top of her head. Lucy blushed.

"Mr. Snippet? Does this plan meet with your approval?" Mr. Little asked.

"It does," said Mr. Snippet firmly.

"Good!" said Uncle Nick. "If we're going to do this tonight, we'd better get cracking."

Everyone stood up and dusted themselves off. At that moment, Cousin Dinky came walking along the pipe.

"So *there* you all are," he said. "Della, Mom, and I arrived a short while ago, and Uncle Pete told us everyone was out sightseeing. I've been all over this house looking for you."

Dinky walked up to the Ground Tinies. "Well, I'll be a son of a gun! Whit Snippet!" He shook the man's hand. "I haven't seen you in a possum's age!"

Whit Snippet smiled a wide and friendly smile. "Brother Dinky, how be you?"

"Oh, you know me, Whit! I'm always out delivering the mail and exploring. It's one wild adventure after another." Cousin Dinky grinned, cocking his thumb back at himself. "After all, Danger is my middle name!"

"So, Dinky," Uncle Nick walked over and put his arm around his nephew. "You call yourself a daredevil adventurer, eh?"

Dinky laughed. "You *know* I do, Uncle Nick," he said. "Why, there's nothing I'm afraid of."

Uncle Nick's smile faded. He pulled Dinky closer, and whispered in his ear: "Well, hold on to your hat and fasten your seatbelt, junior. You're about to have the adventure of a lifetime."

"Where are those girls?" Uncle Nick whispered to Mr. Little. "They should be here with the cheese by now!"

The Littles, Specks, and Snippets were outside on the Biggs' back deck. It was almost midnight on Thanksgiving eve. The Bigg family was soundly sleeping in their beds. They couldn't have known that just outside, in their backyard, a group of tiny friends were about to wage an all-out battle against dozens of hungry field mice.

The only ones who weren't there were Mrs. Little and Granny, Mrs. Speck, and Mrs. Snippet. They had stayed behind in the Littles' apartment. They were making hot cocoa and plates of tiny sandwiches for their family members outside.

Aunt Lily was running back and forth from the apartment to the deck, making sure that everyone had enough food and warm clothing. No one was sure how long this battle would last.

"Let's go down the list and see if everything is in place," said Uncle Nick. He and Mr. Little began walking up and down. They could hear the mice squeaking and scratching on the patio below them.

"Cat food cans," Major Nick Little barked out.

"Check!" said Mr. Little.

"Easy Light charcoal briquettes," said Uncle Nick.

"Check!" said Mr. Little again.

"Matches," called out Uncle Nick.

"Nick," Mr. Little said impatiently, "everything is in place. We're only waiting for the girls to get here with the cheese."

At that very moment, Lucy, Janie, and Annie popped out of the outside electrical outlet door. They came running, each holding a slice of Swiss cheese. The cheese was fluttering out behind the girls like huge, pale yellow wings.

"Good job, ladies!" said Uncle Nick. "Swiss cheese has a nice sharp odor. It should really drive those old mice crazy. Tom, go and see how the Snippet boys are coming along with that fire. Everything should be moving along just as we've planned it. Remember: Timing means everything when it comes to defeating one's enemy!"

Tom Little walked up behind Jeb and Cody Snippet. They were crouching down and furiously rubbing the stems of two wooden stick matches together.

Tom blinked. "What are you guys *doing*?" he asked slowly.

"Your uncle said we should start the fire with these two sticks," said Jeb, the older boy. "They just be starting to smoke a little bit. It not be too much longer now," he said.

Tom tapped the boys on the shoulders, and they stopped their rubbing. "Allow me," said Tom. "Stand back."

He took one of the matches and pushed the head along the deck. The match burst into flames with a crackling noise and a lot of thick, blue smoke.

The Snippet boys fell backward onto their bottoms in surprise. Jeb almost went off the deck.

"Sorry," Tom said and handed the burning match to Cody. "Are you okay, Jeb?"

The Snippet boy nodded his head.

Tom lit the other match and turned to the older boys. "Come on," he said. "Let's get the fires going."

The boys walked over to three cat food cans that were lined up along the edge of the deck. Each can had a small brick of charcoal in the center. The boys lit the charcoal, and covered the cans with a long rectangle of metal screen, cut from an old screen door.

As the charcoal burned, the men removed the labels from three soup cans that they had taken from the Biggs' garbage. Then they used long rubber bands to hold the soup cans together in a row. They also tied pencils across the back of the row of cans.

Finally, the three cans were lifted up and set on top of the screen, with the burning coals beneath them.

All of the people on the deck took turns getting water from the outside water faucet. For buckets they used everything from tiny jelly jars to large, plastic bottle caps. Before long, they had filled the three soup cans about halfway each with water.

"Lucy," called Uncle Nick, "bring the honey!"

Lucy Little struggled to carry over a small squeeze bottle of pure bees' honey. The bottle was shaped like a bear cub, and was almost as tall as Lucy herself.

Uncle Nick and Mr. Little lifted her up. She squeezed the bottle into all three tin

cans, mixing sticky honey with the already-bubbling water.

"Now the cheese!" cried Uncle Nick.

Annie and Janie began tearing small strips from the slices of Swiss cheese. They tossed them onto the patio below. They could hear the mice becoming more excited as they fought each other for the cheese scraps.

"Battle stations, everyone!" shouted Major Nick Little.

Tom and Lucy ran over to an old sling-shot that had belonged to Henry Bigg. Tom had securely tied it to the railing of the deck earlier that evening. Beside the large weapon was a pile of dried beans.

The older tinies all gathered in the center of the deck and waited for Uncle Nick's next order. Everyone was silent. The only sounds were coming from mice noisily chewing on cheese, and the bubbling of the sticky mixture in the tin cans.

Uncle Nick paced up and down in front of everyone. "There comes a time in every tiny person's life," he began, "when he or she must stand and be counted. There is a time when we are all asked to call upon the better nature of ourselves, and defend hearth and home."

At this point, Dinky and Della each took hold of the pencils on either side of the tin cans. Uncle Pete and Stubby Speck stood behind the fires. Each of them held a pencil with the eraser resting against the top of a can of boiling goop.

"There comes a time," Uncle Nick went on, "when each of us must find that towering ten-inch heart that beats inside even the smallest tiny person. There comes a time when everyone needs to do their duty to fight the good fight against the roaming rodent hordes."

He slowly drew his saber from its sheath, and held it above his head. The light from the fires and from the moon glistened on its surface. "And that time," he said slowly, his voice growing fierce and loud, "is *now!*"

He brought the blade of his sword down firmly.

The tinies who were manning the boiling honey and water pushed the cans foward as hard as they could. Sweet-smelling steam filled the air as the hot liquid streamed out. It landed with a loud splash on the patio below.

The mice shrieked and squealed when the hot honey-water hit them. Luckily, they didn't wake up the Bigg family.

All of the mice headed for the woods. One mouse, the very largest of them all, stopped and turned. He looked right up at Lucy, making eye contact with the tiny girl. Lucy recognized him as one of the three mice that had attacked her in the basement.

Quick as a wink, Lucy drew back the slingshot's elastic. Tom placed a single dried bean in the pouch. Lucy counted to three and let go of the elastic. The bean hit the mouse square in the forehead. He flipped over backward, and landed flat on his back. He was out cold.

After a moment, the mouse got up and shook his head three or four times. He looked back at Lucy for a second. He shook his head again and ran chattering toward the woods.

"Take *that*, cheese-breath!" she yelled.

"Lucy!" laughed Uncle Pete. "You literally *beaned* him right between the eyes!"

Lucy thought that was a very corny joke, but she couldn't help laughing just the same.

"Come on, everyone," said Mr. Little, "let's get this stuff cleared away. We musn't leave a trace of all this for the Biggs to find in the morning."

Everyone pitched in, and the deck was cleaned up in no time. Mr. Little, Tom, and Stubby Speck were the last ones still on the deck. They were checking to see that nothing had been left behind.

The air was very cold and the night was very silent. "Good job tonight, men," said Mr. Little. "Let's turn in."

"Turn into *what*?" asked Stubby with a confused look.

"Turn in means go to bed," said Tom.

"Oh." Stubby looked at Mr. Little. "Why didn't you just say hit the hay?"

Stubby took a small bag off of his belt. He pulled out a seed and dropped it off the railing. It broke apart when it hit the patio.

"Pee-yew!" said Tom holding his nose. "Is that what I think it is?"

"Yep," said Stubby. "Old Skunk's smelly stuff. That ought to keep the area mouse free for a good while."

"Why didn't you tell us you had one of your famous stink bombs with you, Stubby?" asked Mr. Little, looking at his friend.

Stubby spit off of the deck. "You didn't ask me," he said. "I'm bushed. Let's turn in."

On Thanksgiving Day, the Littles and their friends went down to the basement to fix the broken window.

The Bigg family had left the house earlier that morning. The tiny people were able to move about easily without fear of being seen. They walked along the water pipe until they came to the stone window ledge where the broken window was. As they peered through the hole in the glass, everyone let out a sharp gasp.

"No! It *can't* be!" Uncle Nick said. "There are more mice outside on the patio than there were last night! There are more mice out there than I've ever seen in one place, outside of Trash City!"

"There must be a hundred of them," said Lucy. "Are they fighting? It looks like they're biting each other."

"Not biting, Lucy," said her father. "They're licking. See how the fur on their backs is all pointed up in little spikes? That's from the hot honey that we poured on them. It might have scared them at first, but now they're back for more. They must like the sweet taste as much as we do."

Sure enough, any mice that weren't cleaning their friends were running their long tongues over the cement patio. They were lapping up every last drop of honey.

"I guess my idea backfired," Lucy said with a frown. "Now we have a bigger mouse problem than ever."

As Lucy spoke, they heard a car door slam from the driveway on the other side of the house. The slam was followed by a series of sharp barking sounds.

"Uh-oh, the terrier!" Mrs. Little whispered to her husband, covering her mouth with her hand in fear. He put his arm around her.

As the tiny people watched, a dog came racing around the corner of the house. It pranced happily around the backyard. The sun shone brightly on its long, black-and-white coat.

"That's no terrier," exclaimed Mr. Little.

"It looks just like a little collie," said Lucy.

"It's a Shetland sheepdog," said Uncle Pete. "They're raised for herding sheep. They're called Shelties."

Suddenly, the dog noticed the huge number of mice. She let out three sharp barks, and began running around the patio in a big circle.

Some of the mice tried to run away, but the dog was closing the circle very quickly. As she ran around and around, the mice began to run in a circle as well.

"I'll be darned," Uncle Pete said. "She's *herding* the mice!"

The frightened mice ran to the middle of the patio. There was a hole in the center for water to drain into after a rain. Now, instead of water, a constant stream of scurrying mice was pouring down into the drain.

When the very last mouse had disappeared down the drain, the dog barked three more times, and wagged her tail. She turned around and looked over at the tiny faces peering back at her from the hole in the basement window.

Before the Littles and their friends had a chance to move, she ran right under the deck and stuck her long, pointy nose through the hole!

Tom Little found himself one inch away from a huge, shiny, black dog nose. For a split second, time seemed to stand still as Tom and the dog looked at one another. Then, it happened. The dog's long, wet, pink tongue lashed out and licked Tom from the tip of his shoes to the top of his head. He fell backward and landed on his rear end. He was soaking wet.

The dog barked happily, and wagged its tail.

"Callie! Callie!" Henry Bigg ran into the

yard, calling to his new dog. "What are you doing under the deck? Come on out here!"

Tom's furry new friend barked at him one more time and smiled a big, happy dog smile. She wiggled out from under the deck and ran back to Henry.

The Littles and their friends watched as Mr. and Mrs. Bigg strolled around the corner of the house. The couple were close enough for the tiny people to hear them talking as they watched Henry and the dog running around in the yard.

"That Sheltie is a beauty," said Mrs. Bigg. "Who would have thought that the runt of the litter would have been the prettiest of the bunch?"

"And because she was so small, she was *free*," Mr. Bigg said to his wife. "That's *my* favorite part!"

"Oh, George!" Mrs. Bigg laughed. "*Stop* it! You know very well I'm good friends with the breeder, and she was happy to give Callie to us."

"This dog is very nice," Mr. Bigg said,

"but she wouldn't know how to catch a mouse if her life depended on it — not like a terrier."

"Still, Henry seems to really love her, so I suppose it was the right choice — even if she'll never be any sort of rat-dog. She's so friendly, she would probably try to make friends with a mouse."

"Or a Little," whispered Lucy as she mussed up Tom's wet hair.

During the rest of the morning, Mrs. Bigg cooked her Thanksgiving dinner and Mr. Bigg watched parades on television. Henry played with Callie until his mother called him inside to eat.

The Littles, the Specks, and the Snippets spent the morning fixing the window. The first job was to get the big piece of glass that Lucy had left on the shelf when the mice attacked her. Tom had used one of Henry's old suction darts tied to a piece of string to pull the glass up off the shelf.

After that, the work went quickly and the window was neatly repaired. For the rest of day, not one squeak was heard from the patio, and no one saw hide nor hair of even a single mouse.

"Oh, boy! The first one's starting! Come on!" Henry Bigg pulled his parents into their living room. They had just finished dinner and were settling down to watch a double feature of great, old monkey movies on TV: *King Kong* and *Mighty Joe Young.*

While Mr. and Mrs. Bigg sat on the sofa, Henry sat on the floor hugging and petting Callie, the latest addition to the Bigg family. She loved the attention. When Henry stopped for a moment to watch the action on the screen, she would stick her long nose under his hand and flip it up in the air. It was her signal for Henry to continue his petting.

Meanwhile, in the kitchen, Mrs. Little,

Mrs. Speck, Mrs. Snippet, and Aunt Lily stood on the kitchen counter, and looked over the leftovers. They directed their families in which things to take, and which to leave behind.

The tiny people took a little bit of just about everything that Mrs. Bigg had cooked for Thanksgiving dinner.

They took sweet potatoes, turnips, and oyster stuffing. Annie and Janie filled plastic bottle caps with mashed white potatoes, gravy, and cranberry sauce. Cody Snippet found a single pearl onion, so gooey with white cheese sauce that it nearly slipped out of his tiny hands. Jeb picked up a half a dozen green peas for everyone to share.

The funniest sight of all was Tom and Lucy Little carrying a slippery turkey drumstick by themselves. They didn't drop it, but by the time they got it to the table, they were so greasy they both had to take a bath and change their clothes.

Finally, the twelve Littles and their eight

visitors from the woods settled down to enjoy their very own Thanksgiving dinner. They were eating in the attic, by candle-light.

The adults and the two Snippet boys sat at a beautiful table. It was an old oakwood skateboard that had belonged to Mr. Bigg when he was Henry's age. Grandpa had made legs for it and polished it until it shone. Everyone sat on benches made from rulers that were tied to the tops of old spools from Mrs. Bigg's sewing room.

Tom, Lucy, Annie, and Janie sat near the adults at Grandpa's card table.

In addition to the leftovers they had taken from the Biggs' kitchen, the feast included food the Tree and Ground Tinies had brought. There were bowls of water-cress salad, acorn meal, honey muffins, and smoked salamander. There were bottles of elderberry wine and blackberry juice.

Ima Speck had baked three fruits-of-the-forest pies. Stubby Speck had a special treat: a single, pickled ear of baby corn for each tiny person at the table. He was very proud to say that he had grown the tiny ears himself in a sunny glade, deep in the Great Woods. As far as he knew, he was the only living person, big or small, who knew that such a place even existed.

"I would like to make a toast," said Mr. Little, who was seated at the head of the skateboard. He raised his glass of elderberry wine. All of the adults raised their wine glasses, and the children raised big mugs of blackberry juice.

"To good — no, to *great* friends. This year, Thanksgiving is more than just a word. Our friends here really deserve great thanks for all the help they've given us and for sharing the bounty of the forest. Here's to the Specks and the Snippets!"

Everyone cheered, and raised their glasses. Lucy Little got up and ran over to her father. She tugged on his sleeve. He bent down, and she whispered something in his ear.

"Oh, yes! Lucy has just reminded me," he raised his glass again. "Here's to our great new friend Callie, the Wonder Dog, and to never, ever, seeing another mouse around here anymore!"

Everyone cheered again, except for the Snippet boys. Cody turned to his brother with a puzzled look on his face.

"Jeb, I thought you said we was going to have honey-glazed mouse for Thanksgiving supper this year!" he said.

"Yuck!" said Lucy.

Cody cracked a sly smile. "Gotcha!" he said.

Everyone laughed. Then they all settled down to enjoy the very best Thanksgiving dinner any of them had ever had.

When the last bit of fruits-of-the-forest pie had been eaten, Cousin Dinky reached underneath the skateboard and pulled out his battered old guitar case.

Cousin Dinky had long considered himself a great musician. The truth was, he was terrible. His family and friends were too polite to tell him just how bad he really was. The only person who truly enjoyed his singing was Granny Little, and that was only because she was so hard of hearing.

"I thought I might entertain everyone with a little number that I just finished writing this very afternoon," said Dinky with a grin.

Uncle Pete's ears perked up. "Whoopsie daisy!" he said, suddenly. "Darn the luck, here we are in the attic, and nature calls. I'll be back in five minutes."

He picked up his cane and quickly limped away. He couldn't stand to listen to Cousin Dinky and made up any excuse to get away before the singing started.

Granny Little turned to the Specks and Snippets. "Oh," she exclaimed, "we're in for a treat! Dinky's just a wonderful singer."

Everyone got quiet as Dinky began to fingerpick a tune on his guitar. He sang in a high, off-key, shaky voice:

I'm just a poor field mouse
Wanderin' through this world;
Ain't got a house
Or a mousie girl.
There's just one thing
Brought me to my knees;
Weren't jewels and rings
'Twas a piece of cheese.
This once proud mouse
Got treated like a mole
When that doggie louse
Chased me down a hole.
Wish I was born
As a dog or cat;
I feel so forlorn
I'm just a dirty rat.

Everybody clapped at the end of the song. Lucy Little clapped the hardest of all. "That was *great*! Didn't you think so, Dad?"

Mr. Little was clapping politely. "Well," he said, "I've certainly never heard him play the guitar so well."

Dinky overheard him. "Thank you!" He grinned. "I've been practicing!"

"Well, I didn't think it was so hot," said Granny Little.

"You *didn't*, Granny?" said Dinky. "I thought you were my biggest fan!"

"I *am*," sniffed Granny. "But when you start writing songs from a *mouse's* point of view, that's where I draw the line!"

"I'm sorry you didn't like that one, Granny," said Dinky. "I have another one called 'My Window's Got a Hole in It.' Shall I play it?"

"*No!*" said everyone at the same time, laughing.

Dinky looked hurt. "What we mean, Dinky," said Mr. Little, "is that it's getting late. Let's clean up, and we'll hear your song later, downstairs."

Dinky brightened up. "Okay," he said. "Sounds good to me!"

Just then, Uncle Pete returned. "I'm back," he said. "Did I miss anything?"

Lucy ran over to her uncle. "You missed Cousin Dinky's mouse song! It was neat!"

"Yes," Mr. Little said, winking at Uncle Pete, "it was a real holiday treat."

"Darn the luck," said Uncle Pete. "Sorry I missed it. Ah, well, there's always next year, isn't there, Lucy?" He mussed Lucy's hair.

"You don't have to wait that long," said Lucy. "Dinky is going to play for us later. If you ask him nicely, I'm sure he'll play the mouse song again!"

"Oh," said Uncle Pete quietly, his face falling. "Oh, goody, goody gumdrops . . ."

Very early the next morning, Tom and Hildy took the Specks and the Snippets back home. The cat was much faster than

Old Skunk. Tom was able to make the trip into the woods and get back to the house before the Biggs even woke up. Hildy hadn't even minded pulling Stubby's covered wagon behind her.

Tom and Lucy spent the rest of the day watching Henry and his new pet playing in the backyard. They watched him through the newly fixed basement window until Mrs. Bigg called Henry to come indoors.

Before they went back into the house, the dog squeezed herself underneath the deck. She looked at Tom through the window, and barked happily. Henry called to her. The dog looked back at Tom Little.

Lucy didn't see it happen, but Tom knows that Callie winked at him and smiled before she ran back to jump into Henry Bigg's arms.

Read more adventures of the Littles
in these books by John Peterson